RELATIVITY
"Township Stories"

Published by Dung Beetle Dramas
an imprint of STE Publishers
4th Floor Sunnyside Ridge,
Sunnyside Office Park,
32 Princess of Wales Terrace,
Parktown 2143
Johannesburg, South Africa

First published in March 2006

ISBN 1-919855-77-7

Series Editor & Dramaturge: Craig Higginson
Cover & Book Design: Adam Rumball
Printed and bound in South Africa by Werners Proof Shop

RELATIVITY
"Township Stories"

WRITTEN BY
Mpumelelo Paul Grootboom
&
Presley Chweneyagae

Foreword

New South African plays are emerging all the time, but few of them are ever published. When they are, they tend to be too expensive for most students, educators and theatre practitioners to afford. The intention of Dung Beetle Drama, a new imprint of STE publishers, is to publish and distribute the best new South African plays at affordable prices. Most of the plays that are produced in South Africa at present are written in English, so many of the plays in this series will be in that language. But we are also going to be publishing plays in other South African languages (with English translations so that those who do not know the language the play is written in can have access to its content).

During apartheid, the monologue tended to prevail in the best of South African drama. Perhaps this was because theatre saw it as its task to create an opposing voice to the dreary but clearly effective monologue of apartheid. To the propaganda of the State, theatre answered with an equally partisan voice of opposition. Of course, the best South African plays during that time were first and foremost about human lives and stories – they weren't mere anti-apartheid propaganda – but it is interesting to note how the monologue prevailed nonetheless.

Much of the best theatre that has emerged in South Africa in recent years (plays like Paul Grootboom and Presley Chweneyagae's *Relativity* and Mike van Graan's *Green Man Flashing*) seems to question the authority of the monological mode. Do they represent a new dialogical form more appropriate to a democracy? It is too early to tell, but it is certainly possible. Certainly, they do tend to question many of our ideas concerning truth, reconciliation, memory, ethical values, social responsibility, etc.

As the Literary Mananger of the Market Theatre, I am constantly on the lookout for new plays that are surprising, that explore new ground in an interesting and challenging way. For the moment, we are tending to move away from the one-person show and are trying to promote plays that dramatise dialogue, conflict, different perspectives. Most of the plays in this series would have been produced by, or would have passed through, the Market Theatre.

The Dung Beetle series aims to help build a national literature for our new democracy – which is not to be confused with a nationalistic literature, of course. If you want to learn more about present-day South Africa, you will want to read these plays.

Craig Higginson
Series Editor and Dramaturge

Relativity was developed through the State Theatre and premiered in the 2005 Grahamstown Festival, South Africa. This version of the play has been prepared for the Market Theatre production in April 2006. *Relativity* was directed by co-writer Paul Grootboom.

CHARACTERS (IN ORDER OF APPEARANCE):

Bongi	Matlakala	Pulane
Molomo	Dorah	Thuli
Rocks	Dan	Mihloti
Ranko	Pelo	Lovemore
Suzie	Mavarara	Jabulani
Uniform	Lungi	Buda
Miss Nkhato	Mamiki	Mavarara
Dario	Thabo	Mhlaba

All sentences that are not in English have been italicised and followed by a translation in English in square brackets.

ACT ONE

PROLOGUE

Music.

A piercing scream from a female voice comes from backstage. The girl, BONGI (eighteen), comes on stage, running here and there, screaming for her dear life. She is panting; her clothing is torn... She takes a centre spot on stage, still panting loudly but no longer screaming. She acts as if she is hiding behind something. A spotlight is on her and it is accentuating her fright... All of a sudden, she acts like the chaser has found her. The lights change again. BONGI runs around and around in large circles. The catching, the screaming, the raping and the killing follow. She is strangled with her G-string. BONGI is miming all this action – she is alone on stage, the killer invisible...

Music fades off when she dies.

BEAT ONE

When the lights come up again we have two or three uniformed cops standing over BONGI's dead body. The two of our story's detectives come through: one is very short (DET. SGT JAMES MOLOMO) and the other very tall (DET. SGT ROCKY MOTSHEGARE). The pathologist, RANKO, is already there.

Rocks	*(To a female uniformed cop)* Suzie!
Suzie	*(With a morning smile)* Hi, Rocks.
Rocks	*O santse o rata banna?* [I see you still love men?]
Suzie	*(Frowns)* Oho!
Ranko	Rocks.
Rocks	Yes, Ranko, howzit?
Ranko	Molomo.
Molomo	Hey!

They shake hands. MOLOMO kneels before the dead body.

Molomo	Does she have a name?
Uniform	We found no documents on her, no ID.
Molomo	Who called it in?
Uniform	Anonymous call.
Ranko	Looks like she was strangled with her underwear.
Molomo	A G-string?
Ranko	Yes. I think the strangler is back in action.
Molomo	I told you Rocks, this is the third body now… I told you we have a serial killer on our hands.
Rocks	We're not sure yet if it's the same arsehole. Let's investigate gentlemen, and not make assumptions.
Ranko	But it's the same modus operandi, Rocks. Same signature.
Uniform	*(Showing them her sandals and a piece of clothing)* We found these on the other side of the bush…
Rocks	What're these?
Uniform	Sandals and a top. Looks like she was being chased around before she was killed.
Rocks	Is that your opinion?
Uniform	Yes, sir.
Rocks	Look here, Constable, if I want your opinion I'll ask for it… but until you pass your detective exam, keep it to yourself.
Molomo	But he's right Rocks – and if that's the case, then it's definitely the G-string Strangler.
Rocks	G-string strangler? You still call him that?
Molomo	What?
Rocks	Do you want us to write reports and investigate a killer, naming him after womens' underwear?
Molomo	Give him a name then.
Rocks	You see, Mouth, just be –
Molomo	Don't call me Mouth!
Rocks	Just because you have a bad name doesn't mean you have to make up for that by giving these killers pathetic names.

Molomo	You're out of line, Rocks, I don't have a bad name!
Rocks	Your surname is a body part! How is that not a bad name?
Molomo	*(Getting angry) Wa itse keng Rocks, re tlo gogana ka dihempe if you go on ka matlhapa a.* [You know what, Rocks, we're going to fight if you go on insulting me like this.]
Ranko	You're out of line, Rocks. My name is also a body part.

RANKO and MOLOMO improvise their protests against ROCKS and ROCKS interrupts/overlaps them, saying…

Rocks	Hey, hey, hey, look here, gentlemen, it's not my fault… I'm not the one who gave you your names. Let's get back to work, please!

ROCKS kneels at the body.

Rocks	So… "Ranko"… When was she killed?
Ranko	It's hard to say, but… I'd say not over twenty-four hours…
Rocks	Was she also raped, like the last one?
Ranko	Yes, she's got semen all over her pubic area… and she's bruised all over.

ROCKS picks up the G-string on her neck and moves off, smelling it…

Rocks	We really must catch this bastard before he becomes a national celebrity.

Soft music.
The two detectives begin to address the audience… The dead body is not cleared but is kept on stage for reference later in the interrogation room.

Molomo	The girl actually turned out to be one Sibongile Mabaso…
Rocks	And with further investigation and with the help of the community, we were able to establish that she was one of those loose girls of the township – one of her neighbours even went to the extent of calling her "a weekend special".
Molomo	In short, we established that she was no stranger of the night – a regular at many of the roughest shebeens of the townships… She is said to have been loud, rude and quite an extrovert.
Rocks	"*Sphaphi*" in vernacular.
Molomo	The killer was getting braver – his previous victims had been shy and afraid of the night.
Rocks	Quiet and almost innocent girls who were easy prey for him.
Molomo	A task team for the killings was formed and Rocks was assigned the lead detective.
Rocks	The behavioural science institute got involved and a psychologist drafted a profile of the killer.
Molomo	After studying the case material, she released the following profile…

A psychologist, MANTOA NKHATO, comes through to recite the profile to the audience.

Miss Nkhatho	A young black male between the ages of twenty and twenty-five. Of slender build. He most probably has a physical deformity or speech impediment… which is probably why he stalks his victims to this bushveld, instead of leading them here with his charisma… With other killers, like Moses Sithole, the victims actually trusted him… where –
Rocks	(*Interrupts*) Moses Sithole promised them work, there was no business of "charisma" with him.
Miss Nkhatho	Whereas, with this one, I believe that… as a

	teenager or in his pre-teens, he was probably teased or shunned by girls of his peer group. The killings are some sort of psychological revenge. And because of this, he probably didn't and still doesn't know how to speak to a girl.
Rocks	Is it possible? I mean township boys think with their dicks. As far as I know, there's abso–
Miss Nkhatho	*(Impatient)* Detective, can I please finish?
Molomo	Oh come on Rocks, let her finish. You'll give out your… your disagreements when she finishes.
Rocks	Who's stopping her? *(And then to MISS NKHATHO)* Go on, go on. We have real work to do after you theorise.
Miss Nkhatho	It is my belief that he will never stop. He can't stop. He is starting to enjoy chasing after the girls. He gets some kind of a rush out of it… You must remember that… most serial killers were exposed to some sort of trauma in their formative years. Direct trauma, such as emotional, physical and sexual abuse to the child. And to escape the memories of their horror, they develop fantasies… violent fantasies where they see themselves as aggressors instead of the victims they actually were. If a serial killer was severely beaten up by his parents as a child, he sometimes fantasises about himself being the abuser. And when the fantasies reach a "boiling point", so to speak, a point where they cause unbearable inner stress, then the killer can be ready to act those fantasies out… In other words, he can be ready to kill. With this one, by pure accident, he found pleasure in chasing her… But the feeling of chasing someone around the bush like a lion chasing after its prey may have been so great that he will have to re-live it every time he kills… he will chase them around like wild game… to re-live and recreate the rush of the first chase…

	Therefore, it is my belief that the next killing is likely to be in this very same location.
Rocks	Night in, night out, we went on a useless stakeout… But the killer didn't strike.
Miss Nkhatho	He was on a cooling-off period. This is when a serial killer somehow manages to deal with his problems and doesn't see murder as his only solution. But it never lasts for long. Sooner or later the urge to kill comes up again. Just as any alcoholic can never go for long without a drink, a serial killer never goes for long without killing.
Molomo	We turned the whole township upside-down, interviewing everybody that fitted the suspect's description. But even with our ten-man task team, we were still too under-staffed to achieve a full and effective investigation.
Rocks	But I remained forever optimistic that we would finally catch the bastard. These idiots cannot run forever. Sooner or later they start making mistakes, careless mistakes… and I was confident that when this one made his inevitable mistake, we'd be right there to catch him.
Molomo	The first suspect we brought in for questioning was one Dario Sephai.
Rocks	A first class criminal… Well, not actually first class in my eyes. He was one of those petty township criminals who get a hard on out of terrorising their communities. I dealt with many of his type every day. They have this boastful and brave exterior, trying to hide what cowards they actually are.
Molomo	Well, unlike my honourable partner here, I was actually not convinced that this Dario Sephai could be the serial killer.
Rocks	I actually wanted a direct confession. Ever since I first started being cop, I realised just how many people got away with murder, got away scot-free

simply because the evidence wasn't enough…
You see, what you have to understand about this
country is how far behind we are, technologically
speaking. We don't have all the hi-tech equipment
and investigating devices that you find in movies
or in the US police services. Down here, if you
don't get a confession, ninety percent of the time,
the suspect will walk.

Music.
*A handcuffed DARIO (twenty-four) is hauled into the
interrogation room by a uniformed cop for the next beat.*

BEAT TWO

The detectives approach him.

Dario	I want my lawyer!
Rocks	Lawyer *se gat*! [arsehole] You think this is the movies?! Huh?! What do you know about lawyers?!
Dario	I know I have my rights.
Rocks	Not in here, you don't! My job is to take all your rights away. You do the crime, you better be prepared to do the time.
Dario	I didn't do anything!
Rocks	You can't lie to me, boy! I have you already figured out. I'm more clever than you! I'm more clever than twenty of your brains put together. *Oska ntlela ka botsotsi ba twobob mo!* [Don't come with useless tricks to me!] Now listen here… I'm going to ask you certain questions… and I want nothing but the truth, otherwise you're going to find out why *ba mpitsa Rocks!* [I'm called Rocks!]
Dario	What questions?
Rocks	Shut up! *Go botsa nna fela mo!* [I'm the only one

Dario	that asks questions here!]
	Jaanong ha go botsa wena fela, Steve Urkell ene o irang mo? [Now if you're the only one that asks questions, what is Steve Urkell doing here?]
Molomo	*Nna ke tla go fa mmago sani! Ke mang Steve Urkell? Hao na mokgwa he? Huh? Mmago ha go ruta maitseo?Huh?!*[I'll show you your mother boy! Who's Steve Urkell? Don't you have any manners, huh?!]

DARIO laughs at him.

Molomo	*Oa tshega? Ke eng, o bona comediane mo?Huh?* [What you laughing at? What, you think I'm a comedian? Huh?]
Dario	*Keng one o batla ke lle? Ha nka se lle grootman, wa nthuba!* [What, you want me to cry? I won't cry, old man, you're cracking me up!]
Molomo	*Rocks! Ako o tswale seo se molomo se, ke tloga ke ntsha mabole yaanong nna! Kea mmona, he's looking for my "deadly uppercut"!...* [Rocks! Please make him shut up, I'll start using my fists now! I can see, he's looking for my "deadly uppercut"!]

DARIO has the biggest laugh.

| Dario | *(To ROCKS)* Where do you get this joker?... |

ROCKS hits DARIO.

Rocks	I SAID, "I'M THE ONLY ONE THAT ASKS QUESTIONS HERE!"
Molomo	*Gata ntja, Rocks! Slaan hom!* [Hit the dog, Rocks! Beat him up!]
Dario	This is police brutality!
Molomo	*Mo gate Rocks.* [Hit him Rocks.] He can't even

	spell police brutality – even if you gave him a month to spell it!
Rocks	Look at her. Are you looking?
Dario	Yes.
Rocks	Why did you kill her?
Dario	Ee, e, e, e, listen here, I don't know anything about her. I didn't kill her!
Rocks	You're lying, *jou vuil pop!* [you dirty bastard!] You were seen beating her up in the street!
Dario	What?!
Rocks	Are you going to deny that?
Molomo	We have witnesses.
Dario	But I didn't kill her.
Rocks	Now listen here… I've got three dead bodies, all strangled with a G-string… How many more are there?
Dario	What?
Rocks	How many more did you kill?!
Dario	You think – *he banna!* [oh my God!] You think I'm a serial killer? Three bodies? With a G-string? What are you saying? I'm not a serial killer, I haven't killed anybody.
Molomo	The night this girl died, she was with you.
Dario	She wasn't with me.
Molomo	That's not what her friend says.
Dario	I don't care what she says, she wasn't with me.
Molomo	*Fok jou!* [Fuck you!]

And then to ROCKS…

Molomo	*Mo gate, Rocks!* [Hit him, Rocks!]
Dario	No, wait… Okay… look… she came to my place, looking for me… I chased her away, I was with someone else. I was with my girlfriend, Matlakala. Why don't you ask her?
Rocks	No, no, she won't work as your alibi. Obviously she's going to protect you. Think of a better lie.

Molomo	This girl, the dead girl… Sbongile Mabaso… you say you chased her away, what time was it?
Dario	I don't know, it was late in the evening.
Molomo	And you chased her away, so that she can get killed?
Rocks	Wait, wait, wait, Mouth… He didn't chase her away, she wasn't killed by anyone else… This arsehole is the killer… This is an open and shut case.
Dario	I'm not a serial killer!
Rocks	Listen here, I'm not going to play games with you. Just tell me why you killed her and the others.
Dario	I didn't kill her! What's your problem? Didn't you hear me, I said –

ROCKS hits him.

Rocks	WHY DID YOU KILL HER?
Dario	You can't beat me up like this, I have rights. I know the law. I can sue you for this!
Rocks	The law doesn't apply on filth like you! Why did you kill her? *(Beat)* Are you going to answer me or do you first want me to light up your balls with a cigarette lighter? Mouth, give me a lighter –
Molomo	Don't call me Mouth!
Rocks	Okay, Molomo… give me a cigarette lighter.
Molomo	*He banna! Laetara ya eng?* [Lighter? What for?] You know I don't smoke.
Rocks	Well, go out and get it for me.
Molomo	Me? Go out and get you a cigarette lighter?
Rocks	That's what I said. This arsehole is going to confess if he doesn't want roasted balls.
Molomo	Wait a minute, Rocks… You don't outrank me. You can't send me like a stuurboy as if I'm your junior. I mean –

Rocks	Fuck it, forget it, I'll get it myself.

ROCKS goes out. Silence for a while. MOLOMO is looking at DARIO.

Dario	*Ee bona, hie… ka le chaela, sfebe sena ha sa bolaiwa ke nna.* [Hey, look here… I'm telling you the truth, this bitch wasn't killed by me.] I didn't kill her! I mean – sure, I beat her up… yes, I admit that… *ek het haar vuil geskop, mara ha a bodiwa ke nna!* [I kicked her to hell and back, but it wasn't me who killed her!] And anyway, if I were to kill anyone I'd use a gun. I'm not a serial killer! I'm very normal, I'm not a mental case!
Molomo	It's not very normal to beat girls up!
Dario	It's only this girl that I beat up. I found her fucking around behind my back! I mean, even yourself, what would you do?
Molomo	You have a history of abuse – you've been charged before for beating people up.
Dario	Yes, well… uhm… I – listen… where I grew up… if you're not tough, if you don't hit first… people will play on your head. But I wouldn't kill anyone, most especially a girl…

Beat. MOLOMO is pensive. ROCKS comes back.

Rocks	Take his pants off!
Molomo	What?
Rocks	Take his pants off!
Molomo	Can we talk first?
Rocks	Talk about what? Take his pants off, I got the matches – do your part!
Molomo	Can we talk in private first?
Rocks	Talk about what?!
Molomo	Look man, I don't think he did it.
Rocks	We talked about this, let's not go back to that.

Molomo	But Rocks, we can't torture him. He didn't do it.
Rocks	Whose side are you? Were you there when this girl was killed?
Molomo	No, but –
Rocks	Then don't say he didn't do it.
Molomo	But he doesn't fit the profile. He's not the serial killer type!
Rocks	Don't come and tell me about a profile, written by some woman who knows bugger all about police work. I've been a cop for over twenty years! And anyway, if he didn't do it, we'll see after I burn his balls... This always works, he won't lie when his balls are being roasted like chicken, he'll tell the truth. Now come on, cuff him and let's take off his trousers.

Music. They manhandle him.

Dario	Wait, wait, wait
Rocks	*Thula!* [Keep quiet!]
Dario	I'm not a serial killer! I didn't do this!
Rocks	*Mo tshware, mo tshware!* [Hold him, hold him!] Mouth!

They cuff him and take off his pants. They burn his balls. He screams and screams. After a while, the music pauses and MATLAKALA (sixteen or seventeen) walks on to the stage. MATLAKALA is dressed in a school uniform and is holding a school bag – she is very, very drunk... She speaks directly to the audience.

| Matlakala | Does anyone here know me? Is there anyone here who thinks he or she knows me? I'm not a philosopher, or an analyst of life... I'm just a daughter of a bitch, just like any other son of a bitch inside this theatre. I drink...I fuck... I lie... I eat... I smoke... I even go to church... sometimes. The only difference between me and |

you is that I can tell you my story. *(Beat)* And because it's *my* story… I can tell it whatever way I want… So… before we go on with the scene that follows this one… *(points behind her to the frozen Rocks and Dario and Molomo)*, we're going to go back in time to several months earlier… Come to my house and hear all proper… hear angel trumpets and devil trombones… You are invited…

Music (the version of the William Tell Overture used in Kubrick's "A Clockwork Orange" during the high-speed sex scene). As the music comes up, the actors unfreeze and set up Beat Three, walking backwards very quickly.

BEAT THREE

Several months before…
   At the KEAGILE house. DAN is in the kitchen. His wife, DORAH, comes through, following MATLAKALA. MATLAKALA comes on the stage with her luggage. DORAH is shouting at MATLAKALA.

Dorah	*He wena sekatana ke wena,* where do you think you're going?! [Hey, you tramp…]
Matlakala	Away! Away from you, away from your shouting, away from this house –
Dorah	And where do you think you're going to go?!
Matlakala	Don't worry yourself, shem. Since when did you start caring?
Dorah	*(Grabs her angrily) O batla go reng?! Yeh?! O bua yang le nna?!* [What?! Don't talk to me in that tone girl!]
Matlakala	*Ntlogele ke tsamaye tuu! Akere hao mpatle mo!* [Let me go, please! You don't want me in this house!]
Dorah	*Don't talk to me like ke gamors fela, nna ke tlao klapa o nnyele girl!* [Don't talk to me like I'm rubbish, I'll hit you until you shit yourself!]

Matlakala	*(Ready to fight) O ka seke. Leka wena!* [Never! Just try!]
Dorah	*Heeee... Utlwang bathong! Dan?! Wa mo utlwa ngwana o wa gago?! O eme okare o sethotsela, o nchebile fela, hao nthuse!* [Heeee... Just listen to that! Dan?! Do you hear this child of yours? You're just standing there like a zombie without helping me!]
Dan	Pule, my baby... why don't we sit down and talk about this?
Matlakala	There's nothing to talk about, Papa... *Ha a mpatle mo. Oa mo utlwa o mpitsa sekatana.* [She doesn't want me here. You heard her, she's calling me a tramp.]
Dorah	*O eng wena?! Hao bone gore o sone. Hao bone gore o iphetotse stratmeit! Ore keng, o nagana gore o mosadi?! Ha se gore hao kreya di-phiriote o mosadi.* [What're you?! Don't you see you are a tramp! You've turned yourself into a streetmate! Or what, you think you're a woman now?! If you get periods, it doesn't mean you're a woman.]
Matlakala	*Oa mo utlwa, Papa.* [You hear that, Papa?]
Dan	*Dorah, lwena ako o eme pele man!* [Dorah, wait a minute man!]
Dorah	*He-e Dan! Don't you dare! Don't you dare take her side! Ke wena o mo senyang ngwana o! Nna ha ke batle ngwana o tlong tlelang ka bofebe ba ko straateng!* [No Dan! Don't you dare! Don't you dare take her side! You're spoiling this child! I don't want a child to come to me with her street whoring!]
Matlakala	*Ha ke sfebe!* [I'm not a whore!]
Dorah	*O setse o itse polo yanong, ebile e go ruta le gore o inkarabisetse!* [You already know a dick now, it's even teaching you to answer back to me!] And I'm telling you, my girl, you'll never amount to anything in life! You'll end up exactly like this...

	what you are… *kuku e e dulang e emetse go jewa!* [...a vagina that's always waiting to be fucked!]
Matlakala	*(Tearfully)* It's okay, it's okay…
Dan	*Pule, ngwanaka* [Pule, my child], running away won't solve anything. I mean, where will you go? *Kaosane re tla be re utlwa gotwe o prostitute yanong…* [Tomorrow we'll start hearing that you're a prostitute…] Please stay, my baby… we can overcome this, you'll get over this… Let's sort out our problems like civilised human beings without screaming about like… like we're coloureds *ba ko* Eldorado Park… [...coloureds from Eldorado Park.]
Dorah	*Dan, nna o satlo mpitsa le-khalati!…* [Dan, don't come and call me a coloured!] I'm not a coloured *nna*! Put some sense into this daughter of yours. *Kgante wena,* [What about you…] what kind of a man are you?
Dan	Now you're getting out of line, Dorah… You can't talk to me like that in front of the child.
Dorah	*Ke reng nna?* [What should I say?] It's your daughter you should be talking to, not me. You're behaving like you're a man only by what hangs between your legs!
Dan	Don't push me, Dorah, don't push me to do something I'll regret!
Dorah	What are you talking about? Your whole life is full of regrets! What, am I too wrong to speak my mind?! You only become a man when you go to the toilet and masturbate.
Dan	*Dorah, o tla tloga o ntena, ke tla tloga ke go khenekha yanong, 'strue's God!* [Dorah, you're starting to piss me off, and I'll beat you up, 'strue's God!]
Dorah	*(Laughing sarcastically)* Heeee! He-he-he! You?! Hit me?! With what?! You can't afford it, man.

	You're unemployed! You won't afford the medical bills or your bail for that matter! You're useless, Dan – you're just like this rubbish daughter of yours.
Matlakala	*Nna ha ke rubbish nna! You're a very bad woman, ebile ha ke itse go tlile yang gore Papa ago nyale!* [I'm not a rubbish! You're a very bad woman, I don't even know how it came about that Papa married you!]
Dorah	*(Slaps her) Hei, voetsek! O mpotsa masepa, jou fokon bitch! Tswa, tswa! Get out of my bloody house!* [Fuck off! You're telling me shit, you fucking bitch! Get out, get out! Get out of my bloody house!]
Matlakala	I was going anyway!

MATLAKALA goes with her bags.

Dorah	*Go, go! Re tla bona gore o tla fella kae! And don't ever come here! Le ka tsatsi la motlholo! Jou fokon bitch!* [Go, go! And don't ever come here! Even if hell freezes over! You fucking bitch!]

MATLAKALA runs off. DARIO's shack is set up…

BEAT FOUR

DARIO is with his two friends – PELO (twenty) and MAVARARA (twenty-two). They are sitting in a street corner, smoking weed and talking.

Dario	*Ek het daai bitch vuil geskop! Vuil, vuil, vuil! Go tswa daar ko Mamikies ne ke mo mathisa mo strateng moen my parabellum tot-tot gore le kuku ya gage ya "one for all" ebe e fufule.* [I gave that bitch a thorough beating! I gave her a chase

with my parabellum from Mamikies until that "one for all" pussy of hers got all sweaty.]

Pelo *Hae, o masepa ntanga… Dario kai one, kai two ke mo fothong! I heard that story, bla yaka!* [You're a bad arse, my friend… Dario only once, for the second time it's only on a photo! I heard that story my friend…]

Mavarara *Watte cherrie is daai?* [Which "chick" is that?]

Dario That bitch called Sbongile.

Mavarara Oooh that one who didn't want you to fuck her the other day?

Dario *Ja, die selde snaai. Le daai tyd a neng a ntshokodisa ke sele ka mo chuma met 'n warm klap ebe ke mo isa gae. Ha ke tlo ncenga nnyo nna!…* [The very whore. Even that time when she didn't want to give out, I hit her with a hot slap and then took her home. I won't beg for pussy.]

Pelo *Ha mare, jy't haar vuil ge-skop Ntanga! I saw her yesterday ka daar ka ko strateng sa bone…* [You gave her a filthy beating my friend! I saw her yesterday at the street where she lives…] I didn't even recognise her – if it wasn't for that unique arse of hers, I wouldn't have known her. You've really re-organised her face, even those sunglasses she had on couldn't hide her ugliness - *omo kobofaditse ntanga!* […you've really made her ugly my friend!]

Dario *Wa nkitse, wa nkitse!* [You know me, you know me!]

Mavarara *Ele gore why omo murile?* [Why did you beat her up?] What did she do to you?

Dario *Ne, o ntlwaela masepa daai hoermeit!* [She takes me for shit, that whore!] I go there ko Mamikies and I find her hanging out with some arsehole – 'n charma-boy wannabee… They were hugging and laughing as if they're in *The Bold and The Beautiful.*

Mavarara	*Kak! Kak! The Bold se gat! Ke kasi hieso!* [Crap! Crap! Fuck "the Bold"! We're in the township here!]
Dario	When I went over there, where they were sitting, and I told that bitch we must go, she answered me like shit, *a ntlolela okare popcorn.* […jumping about as if she's a popcorn] And *daai moegoe* says to me "you heard the lady, she doesn't want to go"… *ka sekgowanyana sa matsatsantsa!…* [And that idiot says to me … with a coconut English!] I hit him with a flying kick before he could even stand up!

PELO laughs excitedly.

Pelo	*I know you ntanga. Jean Clodi Van Deim!* [I know you my friend. You're Jean Claud Van Damme.]
Dario	When he was still trying to recover from my kick, I stepped on his chest, with my 9mm already out!
Pelo	*E, e, e… o mmontshitse movie wena mos?* [You showed him a movie?]
Dario	Now, as I was turning to deal with the bitch, I find out she's gone! I went after her! When I caught her, *ek het hom haar ma ge chee. Hierso, bo di hand. Ha kao chaela, ke mo trapile dik, ka mo tlisa hie, ka mo nyoba dik!* [When I caught her, I beat her up. I'm telling you, I beat her up like crazy, and then I brought her here, and I fucked her like crazy!]

MAVARARA laughs at that.

Pelo	*Haa, mare Ma-D, nke sele wa mo gana! Bullet-out, binne bo daai koek!* [But Dario, you should've shot her! Bullet-out, right inside her cunt!]

Dario   *Hae, nnyo hae ganiwe, bafo, ya jewa! Ya jewa daai ding! Ee, die man! That's why o bolaiwa ke go iskomora so!* [You don't shoot a pussy, man, you fuck it! This guy… that's why you wank all the time!]

MATLAKALA comes through from the opposite side of the street, carrying her bags. MAVARARA is the first to see her, he pokes DARIO to look. DARIO is surprised to see her. He rises and slowly approaches her as she approaches him…

Dario   And then? *Wat gat aan ka di beke?* [What's going on with the bags?]

She is crying. She drops her bags, looking for pity…

Dario   *Wat nou? What jive?* [What now? What's the problem?]
Matlakala   *Ba nkobile ko gae.* [They chased me away from home.]
Dario   *Ba go kobile?* [They chased you away?]

DARIO is surprised and doesn't know what to say. MATLAKALA turns to face the audience…

Matlakala   *(To the audience)* What we do in the name of love… I was fifteen when I first met Dario. He told me that he loved me, and… that I meant the whole world to him. He called me his bitch, *sfebe sa gage* [his bitch]… He was my love, my one and only… I gave up my family in the name of love. I gave up my friends, my future, my everything… all in the name of love.

She and DARIO kiss as the setting is changed to DARIO's bedroom. They get on the bed as they begin foreplay. But before it gets far, MATLAKALA stops him.

Matlakala	Dario?
Dario	Huh?
Matlakala	Wait a minute…
Dario	Huh?
Matlakala	Wait a minute… We can't do this without a condom.
Dario	What do you mean? *O batlo o reng eintlek?* [What are you trying to say?]
Matlakala	Do you have condoms?
Dario	*Ei, ne dile teng daai goetes dibodile.* [They were here those things, but I'm out now.]
Matlakala	What?
Dario	*Di fedile.* [They're finished.]
Matlakala	What do you mean? It means you sleep with other people.
Dario	There's no one else, it's only you. I gave Mavarara my last pack of condoms. Now come on, don't spoil the mood, let's do this…
Matlakala	No, Dario. It's not safe, you sleep with too many girls. If I sleep with you without a condom, I'll be sleeping with all those other girls.
Dario	What other girls? *O batlo reng mara ye?* [What are you trying to say?] There's no other girls! Look, I don't know where you get these crazy ideas but… to tell you the truth, I'm getting fed up – *o tlo nkhenya go sa le early.* [… you're going to piss me off very quickly.] You're the only one I sleep with.
Matlakala	I'm not stupid, Dario. *Kea itse ka Itebeng…* [I know about Itebeng…] She told me about you… I also know that you fuck Pulane, so please don't lie.
Dario	Okay, okay, I admit, I did fuck Itebeng, but I was drunk… she's the one who seduced me… and anyway, we were not that serious by then, me and you… *But Pulane ene, o bua mmage if she says I*

	fucked her! [But Pulane, she's fucking lying if she says I fucked her!]
Matlakala	Yes, but I can't afford to be pregnant, Dario. I have to go to school.
Dario	You won't be pregnant, baby, *otla spanisa di-morning-after.* […you'll use morning-after pills.] And please don't tell me about school, coz it's two months since you've gone to school… and you know you don't like it.
Matlakala	There's this girl at school, she's pregnant now… she used di-morning-after and she's pregnant now.
Dario	She didn't use them correctly. *Sy's dom! Ke sho ene o di spanisitse leite, ka bo ma afternoon ore after two days, ore bosigo bo bo latelang – ene daai ding tsele di bitswa di "morning-after", eseng di "afternoon-after" ore di "night-after" ore di "two days after"…* [She's stupid! I'm sure she used them late in the afternoon or after two days, or the following evening – and those things are called "morning-after" pills, not "afternoon-after" or "night-after" or "two days-after"…]

She has a laugh, despite herself.

Dario   Now come on, we'll argue about this later.

Music.
    DARIO kisses her passionately. They continue making love. This is represented in a non-naturalistic way – as a kind of dance during the scene change.

    DARIO gets an artificial tummy and puts it – as part of the "dance" – under MATLAKALA's dress. After this, she walks to the centre of the stage, a pregnant woman holding her tummy thoughtfully. The lights dim, leaving a spot on her.

Matlakala	*(To the audience)* I lived together with Dario *mo mpantjeng wa gage* [in his shack]. A matchbox shack full of stolen goods. I had everything a girl could want. If I needed anything, Dario would simply steal it for me. Nothing was impossible for him. *(Beat)* It was at this point in my story when Dario got arrested… He was accused of being a serial killer and his balls were burnt… Lucky for him, he had already got me pregnant.

ROCKS and MOLOMO come through and call out DARIO's name.

Rocks	Dario Sephai?
Dario	Yes?
Rocks	Detective Motshegare.
Molomo	Detective Molomo.

DARIO instantly runs, thinking that they want him in connection with one of his many robberies… They chase after him, off the stage… A pregnant MATLAKALA runs after them, shouting out to DARIO.

BEAT FIVE

After the music fades, we find DAN sitting with LUNGI. MAMIKI, the shebeen owner, is arguing with DAN about how DAN still owes her… After a while, MAMIKI goes away. LUNGI is reading a newspaper. There is a girl called PULANE seated with another girl at a different table. At yet another table is a young man (THABO) reading a book and drinking coffee.

Lungi	Hei, look here my friend… They say the G-string Strangler has claimed victim number four…
Dan	Number four? He's getting busy…
Lungi	Why do you think this happens?… I mean, someone going around killing people like this?
Dan	I don't know, bot, that question should be directed to God, not me. All I know is, I hope

they catch him… coz my daughter is out there where I don't know…

A song comes up softly : Satchmo's "Cheek to Cheek".

Lungi　　　Ag, don't worry, they always catch them in the end. *Mina* I don't know why –

Dan　　　　*(Interrupting)* Listen… listen, my friend…

Lungi　　　What?

Dan　　　　The song, the song… You know, this song… *this song e nkgopotsa the first time ke kopana le Dorah*… We were very young then… She was very beautiful, she still is… But that time, *eish, bot… kaochaela man*… that woman was a marvel. *Lerago lele, bot, dirope tsele, bot, matswele ale, bot… ijooo, hao itse niks wena! Marcia Turner bot!* [… this song reminds me of the first time I met up with Dorah… we were very young then… she was very beautiful, she still is, but that time… eigh, bot, I'm telling you… that woman was a marvel. That arse… those thighs… those breasts. You know nothing, you. Marcia Turner, bot!]

He shouts out to the back.

Dan　　　　He Mamiki, Mamiki?! Volume, give me some volume, doll!

The volume goes up and DAN begins dancing. He goes into a flashback-like sequence, where we see him dancing with DORAH like an ace. At a certain point, DORAH moves off and DAN is left standing there like a zombie, as if telling us that that time is now over.

Lungi　　　*(Crossing to him)* Dan?! Danille? Dan?!

DAN snaps out of his trance-like state when LUNGI shakes him.

Dan   It's all gone now… It's gone… The music is over…

Lungi   Cheer up, man, things will come right.

Dan   Come right *kae*, bot?… I've gone through six months without getting any. *Okare ke mo traeleng ko New Lock.* [What do you mean "come right"? … It's as if I'm on a trial in New Lock Prison.] I last ejaculated when I lost my job.

Lungi   *Shapa ma-dice, my friend. Shaya ma-dice. Mina, that's what I do.* [Play the dice, my friend. Play the dice. Me, that's what I do.]

Dan   I'm tired of masturbating, bot! Plus they say it makes you blind.

Lungi   Eee? Is that true? I've been feeling my eyes going bad…

Dan   I don't know what happened, bot… *(He starts to cry)* What happened to this woman? What happened to her motherly love… huh? Her compassion, her… her… eish, bot!… It's all so… so complicated.

He cries and cries.

Lungi   Take it easy, man… It's not the end of the world. Things will come right… Come on, my friend, don't cry… don't cry… *(He tries to speak Tswana; he has a heavy Zulu accent) Mutlugele, mudimu utla mmona…* [Leave her be, God will deal with her.]

They move off and go home.

DAN takes the beer bottle from LUNGI as they start out… Just then, MAMIKI appears.

Mamiki   Heey, Dan! That's my empty!

Dan	It's still full, my dol… I'll bring it tomorrow.
Mamiki	And if you don't come with my money tomorrow don't bother to come at all!
Dan	*Tlogela bo-snakse man!* [Stop being funny!]
Mamiki	*Hai tsamaya!* [Go away!]
Dan	*(As he exits) O snakse man! O snaks! O snaks!* [You are funny, funny, funny!]

After DORAH, LUNGI and DAN exit, MAMIKI is left alone with one patron (THABO, nineteen). She approaches him; he has been immersed in his reading…

Mamiki	And then, *wena*?
Thabo	*(Raising his head)* Huh?
Mamiki	Why are you still here? I'm closing up.
Thabo	I'm still finishing my coffee.
Mamiki	Your coffee? This is a tavern, you know. Why do you want to drink coffee in a tavern?
Thabo	I like being around people.
Mamiki	Well, people are gone. You can go too.
Thabo	As soon as I finish my coffee. I paid for it.

MAMIKI surveys him in silence for a while.

Mamiki	You know, I've seen you around here… You say you like people, but I've never seen you talking to anyone.
Thabo	I said "I like *being around* people"; I never said "I like people".

Beat.

Mamiki	You sound intelligent. What are you reading?
Thabo	*Jack and the Beanstalk.*
Mamiki	Ooh, I see… we have Bill Cosby here.
Thabo	I'm not joking, it's the truth.
Mamiki	Let me see.

Thabo	No, you won't like it… It's a pornographic novel, not the common fairytale… The beanstalk is Jack's phallic instrument, you know, ehm –
Mamiki	Spare me the details.

She sits down. She lights herself a cigarette.

Mamiki	What's your name?
Thabo	Thabo.
Mamiki	You sound like someone very intelligent. Are you a university scholar or anything like that?
Thabo	Anything like that.
Mamiki	I was a scholar myself… Didn't finish though… And now, look at what I am… A doctor of the liquor business. *(Beat)* Why do you read pornography? Do you have a girlfriend? *(He hands her the book)* It's not pornography at all… *Catcher in the Rye*… JD Salinger… I've never seen this one before.
Thabo	Famous book.
Mamiki	So… do you or don't you?
Thabo	Don't what?
Mamiki	Have a girl.
Thabo	No, I've never met anyone good for me…

THULI enters.

Thabo	*(Aside)* Until now.
Thuli	*Mama, ke ilo robala.* [Mama, I'm going to sleep.]
Mamiki	Sharp, my baby. Goodnight. Come on, give me a hug…

As she stands to hug THULI, everybody except THABO freezes.

Thabo	There was nothing really special about her… But from that moment, I could write ten to forty

poems about this girl... She was oozing with purity, cleanliness, something you just want to lock away in a Consol glass and observe and scrutinise for eternity... My Eve minus the Forbidden Fruit...

They unfreeze and hug.

Mamiki   Night.
Thuli   Night, Ma.

THULI moves off.

Mamiki   That's my daughter, you know.
Thabo   What?
Mamiki   I saw you. That look... I don't like it.
Thabo   If you don't want us to look at her you should stop her from working in such a place.
Mamiki   She's everything to me. I want her to be the best of what I could never be.
Thabo   You must really love her.
Mamiki   Yes, that I do. She's a gem. So stay away from her. *(Beat)* How old are you?
Thabo   Nineteen.
Mamiki   You're younger than I thought.
Thabo   How old are you?
Mamiki   Don't you know you're not supposed to ask a lady such a question?
Thabo   You must be fifty then.
Mamiki   Oh no – fifty? How cruel. How can you choose such an age for me?
Thabo   How old then?
Mamiki   Let's just say I'm way younger than fifty... and way older than my daughter. *(Beat)* What about some music, Mr Academic?
Thabo   Music?

Mamiki	Yes…
Thabo	Sure.

Music comes up. Marvin Gaye's "Sexual Healing". MAMIKI dances seductively.

Mamiki	You know, when this song plays… it takes me far, far away to special places… When it plays, I just feel… this feeling…
Thabo	What feeling?
Mamiki	Of dancing with the right man. Come on, come on, let's dance.
Thabo	No…
Mamiki	Come on… Don't be shy. I'll lead you. Come on, humour me…

She manages to get him dancing. They dance and then she kisses him. He is highly surprised. She is panting, though. She kisses him passionately. He decides to fall into it. She throws him on the chair and tears her blouse open.

Thabo	Wait a minute.
Mamiki	Shhhhhh… don't speak!

She climbs on top of him and kisses him again. She stands up after a while and begins undressing him until he is in only his shorts and vest. The bed is moved to a more central position and MAMIKI's bedroom is set up. We now have both the shebeen area and the bedroom on stage. MAMIKI and THABO go into the bedroom and they fuck under the sheets.

After the fucking, MAMIKI gets out the bed and puts on her morning gown.

Mamiki	Shuu… That was… that was something else… I think I need a cigarette.

She has a smoke. She looks at him for a while.

Mamiki   *Mara wa itse gore o monate byang?* [Do you know how delicious you are?]

He says nothing.

Mamiki   But don't let that go to your head. It's nothing you did. It's just… actually, I don't know what it is… Maybe your thing, it's not big that it can hurt, and yet… it's not small that it can tickle… It's just… *perfect*. A perfect fit. Or maybe it's not your thing… It's you… Maybe you're just perfect… A perfect… fit. Huh? I was married, you know. Divorced now. There was just something in that marriage that nearly made me hate sex. But now… I remember why it's such a –

THULI's voice comes from off-stage.

Thuli   Mama?

She throws THABO off the bed, to the side where he won't be seen. THULI walks in.

Thuli	Mama?
Mamiki	I told you to knock before you come in here!
Thuli	There's someone at the door. It's the police. They want to speak to you.
Mamiki	What do they want?
Thuli	I don't know.
Mamiki	Ag, they must catch this killer and stop bothering me!
Thuli	What must I tell them then?
Mamiki	Okay, okay, let's go, let's go.

She walks off with THULI. Music.

Thabo	What a talker… I knew it right away: she was in love with me, and here I was, in love with her daughter… There's a psychological term for people who sleep with someone just because they want to get closer to someone else who happens to be closest to that someone… Maybe that's what was happening to me, I thought at that moment… I had slept with the mother just to get closer to her daughter… I don't know what the term for that is, but I'll call that "alternative affection"… That's what my father suffered from…

The lights dim in MAMIKI's bedroom and come up in the shebeen area. MAMIKI is talking to the detectives.

Mamiki	This is a classy place, detective… I serve only the best-mannered people.
Rocks	Manners and alcohol don't go together.
Miss Nkhatho	We believe the killer may be one of your clients, and we're here to see if –
Mamiki	*(Interrupting)* My clients? I serve only the best. This is a classy place.
Miss Nkhatho	Why, do you know all your clients?
Mamiki	Not all, but I know most of them.
Miss Nkhatho	There you go… You see, you can't control whoever comes in here. A killer could come in here unseen.
Rocks	*(Impatient, upstaging Nkhatho)* Look, lady, just supply us with the names and addresses of all your clients so that we can talk to them!
Mamiki	Do you have a warrant?
Rocks	A warrant? For what? Listen here, woman, we don't need a warrant to get names from you… Either you give us the names or we detain you for a while until you give them up.

Mamiki	That would be police harassment. I'm well versed on the law.
Rocks	Look here, you don't want to be telling us about warrants… If I have to come with a warrant, I'll come with a lot more warrants for many other criminal activities that go on in your place…
Mamiki	I have nothing to hide. And I'm not scared of the police… My ex-husband used to be one. If you don't have a warrant then get the hell out of my place before I sue you for trespassing and police harassment.
Molomo	*(Trying to intervene)* No, no, listen –
Rocks	*(To Mamiki)* Are you threatening me?! Coz if you are I'll arrest you, right now on the spot!
Mamiki	I'm not scared of you, detective!
Molomo	Rocks, wait!
Rocks	*(Threatening, overlapping Molomo)* You're not scared of me?
Molomo	Rocks, please, let me handle this.
Rocks	There's nothing to handle, Mouth. This woman thinks –
Molomo	Wait, wait! Rocks, you're not making things easy for us. Please, stay back… I'll handle this.
Mamiki	Look, I'm not giving you any names. Come with a warrant before you talk to me. This a classy place, I don't serve killers here!
Molomo	I know, I know, but –
Rocks	Let's just arrest this slut and get the names from –
Mamiki	Hey, hey, I'm not a slut! Who are you calling a slut?! Go and call your whoring wife a slut!
Rocks	*(Charging her, offended)* What?!
Molomo	*(Blocking him off)* No, no, Rocks, wait!
Miss Nkhatho	*(Overlapping with Rocks)* What is this now?
Rocks	*(Overlapping with Miss Nkhatho)* Did you just call my wife a slut? *(To Molomo)* Let me go, Mouth!

Molomo	No, no, but wait, Rocks… You called her a slut first.
Rocks	She *is* a slut. She's a bitch. What's wrong with calling her what she is?
Mamiki	Hey, *mina* I'm not a bitch! It's your wife you're talking about! Your wife, your mother, your grandmother all combined together! Go call them bitches before –

ROCKS lunges at her before she can continue and grabs her by the throat… He has already drawn his gun and has put it to her head.

Rocks	Do you know my wife?! Do you know my wife?!
Molomo	*(Trying to pull ROCKS back)* No, Rocks, no… Put the gun down.
Miss Nkhatho	*(Also trying to help)* Detective, let her go!
Molomo	Back off, Rocks!
Rocks	Do you know who my wife is, you fucking bitch?! Huh?! Do you know her?!
Molomo	Let her go, Rocks… Please!

Just then, THABO walks in. ROCKS is shocked to see him.

Rocks	Thabo?

He lets go of MAMIKI. THABO passes them, picking up his steps as he goes…

Rocks	Thabo?!

As THABO runs off, ROCKS runs after him… It is as though ROCKS has seen a ghost.

Miss Nkhatho	Who's that?
Molomo	I think… I think it's his son.
Mamiki	*(Surprised)* His son?
Miss Nkhatho	*(To Mamiki)* Are you okay?

Mamiki   *(Pushing her off in anger)* I'm fine, I'm fine!
Miss Nkhatho   *(To Molomo)* Jesus! What's his problem?

MOLOMO starts out… MISS NKHATHO follows him, saying…

Miss Nkhatho   He's a mental case – he shouldn't be in charge of
            such an investigation…

Music for scene change.

BEAT SIX

Flashback…
    *A montage of shots relating THABO's story from birth until when
he's around thirteen years old:*

*1. We see ROCKS and his pregnant wife, MIHLOTI, in their loving
(flowery) moments. MIHLOTI suddenly goes into labour and ROCKS
takes her to the bed to deliver the baby.*

*2. The doctors come through after ROCKS puts MIHLOTI on the bed.
MIHLOTI is screaming as the two doctors help her deliver. They shout
and shout "push-push". After they remove the artificial belly, a smiling
ROCKS emerges from behind the bed with his infant son, THABO…
The artificial belly has been switched for the actor playing THABO.*

*3. ROCKS and MIHLOTI move forward to centre stage with his wife,
MIHLOTI, as they play with the infant son in ROCKS' hands.
ROCKS puts the boy down and the boy starts to crawl away, like a
one-year-old baby.*

*4. When the boy comes back to ROCKS and MIHLOTI, he is now
starting to walk. ROCKS catches the boy before he falls. MIHLOTI
moves away to get a tricycle for the child (who is now around three or
four). She gives the tricycle to the boy and the boy moves off to play
with friends. THABO's friends are playing cars with beer crates
around the stage.*

5. *When THABO comes back, his family moves to centre spot and they begin miming a ride in a car. THABO's childhood friends play around with the crates, and when they crash the crates together, THABO's family falls over – as if in a car crash.*

6. *ROCKS rises from the wreckage and picks up his wife (the only one seriously wounded) and takes her to the bed, where doctors attend to her. They cover her with a white cloth and put her on the stretcher. As they move off stage with her, ROCKS and THABO are crying for her.*
    The scene is then transformed for the following beat…
    It is important to note that all actors in the cast are involved in this scene change. They remove tables as if they are children playing with car wheels, etc.
    Thirteen-year-old THABO is being interrogated by his father, ROCKS, in their house.

Rocks	Thabo?
Thabo	*(Scared)* Papa?
Rocks	What's going on?
Thabo	Papa?
Rocks	*Ke go botsa potso man! Keng, hao nkutlwe?* [I'm asking you a question! What, don't you hear me?!]
Thabo	*Kea go utlwa, Papa.* [I hear you, Papa.]
Rocks	Then answer me… What's going on with you?
Thabo	What's going with what Papa?
Rocks	I was with your teacher today – MaKutu. She was complaining about you. She says you show no attention at all in your schoolwork. She says you sometimes sleep in class, and that you're always absent-minded and that you're failing your tests. She also says you're the brightest kid in the school and if this goes on, you're soon going to be the dullest… a dunderhead… *'n domkop… And ha kena ngwana wa domkop nna… Keng?! Hao batle skolo?!* [And I don't have a dunderhead for a child. What, don't you want school any more?!]

Thabo	*He-e Papa.* [No Papa.]
Rocks	*(Fiercely) Yeh, ore he-e?!* [What, did you just say no?!]
Thabo	*(Sobbing) He-e Papa, ha kere he-e, ka se batla, Papa.* [No Papa, I didn't say no. I want it Papa.]
Rocks	*Yanong keng?* What the hell is going on?! *Keng okare otla iphetola setlhoko tsebe yana? Heh?!* [Now what? ... Why are you turning yourself into a problem child?!]

THABO is crying.

Rocks	Stop it! Stop it, *o llelang*?! Huh?! Are you a girl?! *O shapilwe ke mang?! Ore o batla ke go shape gore o lle sentle?!* [Stop it! Stop it, what are you crying for?! ... Who hit you?! Or do you want me to hit you so that you can cry for the right thing?]
Thabo	*He-e.* [No.]
Rocks	*Yanong keng?!* Why are you crying?! Huh?! Thabo?! [Now what?! Why are you crying?! Huh? Thabo?!]
Thabo	Papa?
Rocks	I'm talking to you!
Thabo	Papa?
Rocks	Why are you crying?!
Thabo	*Papa akere wena ha ke bala o tla mo gonna,* [Papa, when I sleep you come to me and again you hit me]... and... and... you hurt me... *o nkutlwisa botlhoko kana she...* [oh, you are hurting me] Sometimes, sometimes when I think of coming home, I get... I get this feeling... this feeling of not coming home... MaKutu always asks me what's wrong and... and I feel like telling her... I feel like telling her the truth... *gore wena o nkutlwisa botlhoko ha ke robetse... gore wa ntshwara...* [that you hurt me when I'm sleeping... that you touch me] and I don't like

	how you touch me… and… that you don't… you don't love me…
Rocks	Okay, okay Bigboy…
Thabo	*Hao nrate, Papa –* [You don't love me, Papa –]
Rocks	*Ha se jalo "the Great"…* [It's not like that "the Great"…] …Please chana man… Don't go telling people that I don't love you… telling them about these things… you haven't told her anything, have you?
Thabo	*Mh-hm Papa. Ha ka molella, mara… mara…* [No Papa. I didn't tell her, but… but…]
Rocks	Easy chana… it's not that I don't love you, my boy… it's just that Papa o misa Mama… Do you understand?… huh?… You know I wouldn't hurt you… I just forget myself… I miss your mother too much… I can't bear the thought that I'll never see her again… I'm always waiting for her but she never comes…
Thabo	He-e Papa, please don't touch me…

Music. The ghost of MIHLOTI enters

Rocks	Easy, Bigboy… You know I love you. It's just that I miss your mother. I miss everything about her. I miss her cooking, her smile, her eyes… her voice. *(To MIHLOTI)* Howzit baby?
Mihloti	Hallo, my love.
Rocks	Oooh, it's so good to see you again.
Mihloti	Yes, yes, same here, my pumpkin…
Rocks	And your voice, too… Oh, it's wonderful to hear it… Why did you have to go, baby? Why?
Mihloti	I'm not gone… I'm with you. I'll always be with you.

She starts to move back, starting out of the stage.

Rocks	Mihloti? Don't go!
Mihloti	I love you.
Rocks	Don't go… Mihloti!

By this time he is fondling THABO.

Thabo	Papa? Papa? Please don't touch me like this…
Rocks	(*Simultaneously*) Mihloti? Mihloti? Mihloti please don't go like this…

But MIHLOTI is gone…THABO snaps his father out of this trance. Music ends abruptly.

Thabo has stood up from the chair and is now standing away from his father.

Rocks   Sorry, sorry, Bigboy. I didn't mean it… I'm so sorry… I'll never do it again… You don't need to tell anyone about this. Not even your teacher, MaKutu. She doesn't need to know coz Papa is going to search for help. I'll never do this to you again. Now come, go to sleep, there's school tomorrow… *Ala o robale.* [Lie down and sleep.]

Music.
    THABO prepares his blankets. He undresses until he is in his jockeys and gets under the blankets to sleep. A tormented ROCKS is in the background, looking worriedly at a distance. When the boy is snoring, ROCKS approaches him. When he's standing over the boy, a tear drops down his cheek. He begins to undress himself until he is in his BVDs. He slowly gets under the blankets with THABO, trying not to wake him. He then slowly fondles him. ROCKS is crying, as if feeling guilty for what he finds himself doing. THABO wakes up.

Thabo   *Papa he-e! Papa ntlogele!* [Papa no! Please leave me alone!]

THABO cries again.

Thabo   *O rile oka se tlhole o ntshwara gape… ntlogele papa…* [You said you wouldn't touch me again… leave me alone papa.]

He rapes the boy, saying:

Rocks   *(spiritually tortured)* Sorry, Bigboy… Sorry, my boy… *Skalla sani… Papa wa o rata, wa utlwa chana?* [Don't cry my son… Papa loves you, you hear chana?]

Blackout.

BEAT SEVEN

A very drunk DAN and LUNGI are going home, drunkenly singing a Zulu song, "Sandisa nge Cadillac". When they get to a certain point, they go their separate ways.

Lungi   Tomorrow, Dan!
Dan   Tomorrow! Remember, *no dice* – you go blind!
Lungi   I'm drunk now – and you know drinking, it gives you the desire. I'd rather go blind!

He walks off. When DAN gets to his house, he finds a guy called LOVEMORE waiting there.

Dan   And then?
Lovemore   Howzit, my friend?
Dan   What are you doing here?
Lovemore   You don't remember me? My name is –
Dan   I don't care what your name is. What I want to know is what you're doing in my house at this time of the night when I'm not here.
Lovemore   Look, I work with your wife. We've met before. My name is Lovemore Kata.

Dan	*Motlholo… Dorah?! Dorah?! Lekwerekwere le le batlang mo gaka bosigo jaana?!* [Dorah?! Dorah?! What is this "*kwerekwere*" – derogatory name for a foreinger – doing in my house at this time of the night?]
Lovemore	No, no, no, no, my friend, don't call me a *Makwerekwere*. I'm a Malawian. I come from Malawi – I don't know a country called *Makwerekwere*.
Dan	What do you want here?!
Lovemore	I told you, I work with your wife!
Dan	This is not where she works, this is my house!
Lovemore	Wait a minute, my friend, I think you've had a bit too much to drink.

The furniture movers, JABULANI (thirty) and BUDA (thirty), come through, carrying heavy household items.

Dan	Hey, hey, wait a minute… What's going on here?
Jabulani	*Jonga la ndoda, asibizwanga huwe, asizanga kuwe! Siyeke sisebenze ndoda! He Buda, mas'hambe!* [Look here, man, we were not called by you and we're not here for you! Leave us to do our job. He Buda, let's go!]
Dan	*Haowa, madoda… madoda?* [No, guys… guys?]

They go out. Frustrated, DAN turns back.

Dan	*Mara go etsagalang ye?* [What's going on here?]

DORAH comes through with her bags.

Dan	Dorah? What is this? What's happening?
Dorah	I'm leaving you, Dan.
Dan	Lea… leaving me? Wha… what do you mean?
Dorah	This is Lovemore, I'm going to live with him from now on.

Dan	You're leaving me?! For a *kirigamba* [foreigner] called Lovemore?!
Lovemore	Wait a minute with those names, my friend. I don't want to get angry.
Dan	Get angry?! Get angry with who?! Get angry in my house?!
Dorah	Stay in your house then. Come on, Lovemore, let's go.
Dan	Wait, wait, wait, Dorah, wait. Let's talk about this…
Jabulani	*Sisi? Sithatha konke mos?* [My sister? Do we take everything?]
Dorah	Yes, yes, all of it.
Dan	What?!

They take the furniture. DAN stops them.

Dan	*(To the movers) He lona, tlogelang daai goetes, letla bona masepa!* [Hey, hey, leave those things alone, if you don't want trouble.]
Dorah	*Batlogele, Dan, ha osa batle ba ditseye ka fose!* [Leave them Dan, if you don't want them to use force.]

He leaves them and turns to DORAH. They exit with the furniture.

Dan	No man! *Ema pele, Dorah.* [Wait a minute, Dorah.] You can't take away the furniture… I contributed a lot in buying these things.
Dorah	*E kebe ele kgale ba di tsere!* [They could've long been repossessed!] They were once yours now they're mine. You only paid the deposit.
Dan	*Mara Dorah o tsenwe ke eng ye?* [Dorah, what's gotten into you?]
Dorah	*O kolobe! Ke batla go go bontsha gore o kolobe…o kolobe Dan, ke batla go go tlogela ka yona hoko e ya gago…* [You're a pig! I want to

	show you that you're a pig, I want to leave you in this pig sty of yours.]
Dan	Mare Dorah why are you doing this to me? What have I ever done to you to deserve this?

BUDA and JABULANI walk back in for more furniture.

Dorah	You broke your promise, Dan. You promised me bliss, you remember? *O ntshepisitse magodimo le mafatshe*, but instead all I got was a limp dick. [You promised me the world and heavens...]

BUDA and JABULANI laugh.

Buda	*(As they pick up more furniture)* Limp dick – did you hear that?
Dan	What you're doing is wrong, baby. How can you talk like that to me in front of people? *O batla gore ba ntseye yang...* [You'll make them disrespect me...]
Dorah	It's the truth, Dan. You have nothing to offer except empty promises. Lovemore is more of a man than you'll ever be.
Dan	Yes, what do you expect, he's a *kirigamba*! These people use powerful herbs to enlarge their dicks! You can't compare me to *lekwerekwere*!

LOVEMORE grabs DAN angrily.

Lovemore	I will kill you, I will kill you, I will bash your face in!
Dan	Don't touch me, don't touch me!
Dorah	No, no, Lovemore, let him go. He's just a tired joke, you don't even need to do anything to him. Let him go.

LOVEMORE lets him go.

Dan　　　　　I'm not scared of you! I'm not scared of you! Come, come!

Dorah　　　　Don't mind him, sweetheart. You have nothing to prove to him. You've already proven it to me – in bed, unlike him. Come on, let's go.

They take the bags and go.

Dan　　　　　*(Going after them)* Dorah? Dorah? Dorah? *(Crying)* Okay, go! Go, go, go! *O nagana gore ke tla go ncenga! Tsamaya man! Nka se go llele nie!* [You think I'm going to beg you! Go, man! I won't cry for you!] And when things go bad for you don't come back here, I won't be waiting! Go, go, go!

He stops near the door and collapses to the ground, crying like a baby. BUDA and JABULANI come back for the last item, a table. DAN quickly rises and gets on top of the table as they try to take it.

Buda　　　　　Hey, get off that table, *wena*, otherwise it's not only your dick that's going to be limping!

Dan　　　　　*O bua masepa, jou bleksem!* [You talking shit, you rubbish!]

He shouts out to the departed DORAH.

Dan　　　　　*Wa utlwa yanong Dorah gore o nthogisa ka di vuilpop!* [Dorah, you see now that you're making this trash insult me!]

Buda　　　　　*Ke mang vuilpop wena?* [Who is trash?] Get off the table!

Jabulani   Don't talk to him, Buda!… *Masi mthulule!* [Get
                him off!] *(DAN clings onto the table)* Tip him
                off, tip him off!

*They tip him off the table and he falls hard onto the ground. He stays
there. BUDA and JABULANI exit. DAN rises slowly. In silence, he
walks off and starts singing a Satchmo song as he slowly goes off :
"Nobody knows the trouble I've seen."*

End of Act One.

ACT TWO

BEAT ONE

Music.

DARIO is hitting a pregnant MATLAKALA. This is done all over the stage – it must look very cruel. The dialogue is improvised. DARIO is saying very little. After a while, DARIO freezes and MATLAKALA delivers a monologue to the audience.

Matlakala   *(To the audience)* His balls had healed. He was out almost every night, fucking around. When I complained to him, he didn't listen. It was as if he didn't care. And because of that, I also started going out, hanging out with my friends, spending as much time away from my new home. He warned me about this, but I wasn't prepared to be the stupid housewife, who stays at home, reading Bona magazines and gossiping about neighbours with other neighbours. So I went out with my friends. We went to parties, we went everywhere... I didn't care about my showing tummy, I just went everywhere and I had fun... And that's why he beat me up. He found me at my friend Patricia's house, and he beat me up all the way home... As if trying to embarrass me in front of people... *(Beat)* After beating me up like that, strangely, the baby survived... I resented that fact. I felt he no right beating me up that way and still having his baby survive it. How could God be so cruel? How could God make him so happy?

She removes the artificial belly.
Music.

The house has been set up by now and it is a mess… MATLAKALA sits down, crying for a while. She then stands up and starts cleaning up. Her father walks in.

Dan   Matlakala?

Matlakala   Papa? What are you doing here?

Dan   I uh… I came to see you, my baby.

Matlakala   Who told you where I was?

Dan   That friend of yours – what's her name? Patrick, or something…

Matlakala   Patricia?

Dan   Yes… Patricia… *(Attempting a joke)* Even though she's ugly enough to be a Patrick herself.

MATLAKALA smiles.

Matlakala   *Ei wena*, Papa… I'm sorry, the house is a mess.

She tries to tidy up.

Dan   You sound sick. What's wrong?

Matlakala   Nothing. I'll be fine.

Dan   I heard you were pregnant… You don't look pregnant.

She sits on the couch crying, all of a sudden.

Matlakala   I… I lost it. I lost the baby.

Dan   What? How?

Matlakala   He beats me… He sleeps around… He's never home, Papa… I killed the baby. My own baby. I killed her. I killed my own child just to get back at him. I… I killed her.

Dan   Ooh, my baby… What are you doing to yourself? Is this what you want? Look at you… just look at you. I mean, young as you are, living with a man

	under one roof? At your age? He-e, my baby… You're leaving with me, we're going home…
Matlakala	No Papa, I can't. I can't leave… And besides, Mama doesn't want me back.

Beat. DAN turns pensive.

Dan	You mother is not home. You have nothing to worry about.
Matlakala	What?
Dan	Yes, she left me. Your mother left me for a *kirigamba* from Malawi. After fifteen years of marriage! Fifteen years!
Matlakala	Oh, I'm sorry Papa.
Dan	It's okay. I'm a man. I'll get back on my feet again. *(Beat)* She even took my furniture with her. The house is empty now, I'm all alone there. I hear voices… I think I'm going mad… Please come back home, my baby… please… I miss you.
Matlakala	I can't.
Dan	Yes, you can. This is no life for you… I've stopped drinking, I'm busy looking for a job again… I'm trying to get my life into gear… Come and live with me.
Matlakala	Dario won't allow it, Papa. I've threatened to leave him before… he said he'd kill me. He's a dangerous man, he's a criminal. He hijacks cars, he kills people!
Dan	We'll go to the police. We'll make a plan… I'll protect you, my baby. I'll protect you. Please come with me.

Dario enters.

Dario	*En nou wena?* [And now?]

DAN is shocked to see DARIO in actual person.

Dan Hi, bot! Howzit?

Dario *Wat soek jy?!* [What do you want?]

Dan Uhm… *(laughing nervously)* It's a nice place that you have here.

Dario What do you want here?

Dan Well, you see, bot, I'm… well, I'm Matlakala's father.

Dario *Eh monna, o batlang hie?!* [Hey man, what do you want here?!]

Dan I was just here to see how Matlakala is doing… Uhm… Ja. But, it's okay… I'll… well, I'll come at another time.

He starts to go but DARIO stops him. He is shit scared when he is stopped like this.

Dario Hey, hey, hey… Where do you think you're going? What're you doing in my house?

Dan I was – I was – well, uhm, bot… you see, I was – I was just here to see… to see Matlakala… to see how she's keeping.

Dario *O kile wa mpona ke ile ko wena ke ilo cheka jou vrou?* [Have you ever seen me at your house, visiting your wife?]

Dan Uhm… well, no. But, bot, you see… the thing is –

Dario What the fuck are you doing here then?

Dan Okay, okay… you don't have to fight, bot. I was leav –

Dario *(Grabs him by the shirt)* Fight? Fight with who?

Dan No, no, uhm… I'm sorry, bot.

He lets him go.

Dario Listen here, ne… Go! *Vaya hie! Fela pleke!* [Get

	out!] And if I ever again, I'm going to cut your dick off! *Verstaan my?* [Understand me?]
Dan	*Ja, ja, sure. Dankie bot!* [Yes, yes, sure. Thank you, brother!]

DAN rushes off.
  Music.

BEAT TWO

The tavern is set up. THULI is busy studying. After a while, THABO walks in.

Thabo	Hi.
Thuli	We're not open yet.
Thabo	What's that?
Thuli	Who – I said, we're not open.
Thabo	Physical Science? Is it hard?
Thuli	Yes… uhm… actually, I don't know why I had to do it, I should've done History or – look… who are you?
Thabo	I also used to hate it in high school, but now I'm obsessed with it. I can help you if you want.
Thuli	Help me? Who are you?
Thabo	I just want a drink. I wanted to sit and drink and read, but it's okay, I'll help you instead.
Thuli	No, no, I'll be okay… We're not open yet.
Thabo	Okay, I'll wait. What time do you open?
Thuli	But you can't wait in here.
Thabo	I won't be in your way. You can do your Science, I won't – *(Beat)* Where's your mother?
Thuli	My mother?
Thabo	Yes.
Thuli	Do I know you?
Thabo	Yes, you served me coffee the other day, and you told me that –

Thuli	No one comes to a shebeen to drink coffee.
Thabo	And I told you –
Thuli	There's a first time for everything.
Thabo	And then you said –
Thuli	How do you read with so much noise?
Thabo	And I said –
Thuli	I hate silences.
Thabo	And you said –
Thuli	You're strange.
Thabo	And I said –
Thuli	I'm Thabo.
Thabo	Yes, and that… you're beautiful.
Thuli	I don't remember the beautiful part.
Thabo	Well, I do… *(Beat)* You are, you know.
Thuli	No, I'm not.
Thabo	Okay then, you're ugly.

She laughs.

Thuli   No, I'm not!

Just then, MAVARARA walks in.

Mavarara   Holla.

No one replies.

Mavarara   *(Kissing THULI on the cheek)* Howzit, baby? *Ke vraza ho o bona.* [Can I talk to you?]

Thuli   I'm busy.

Mavarara   What?

Thuli   I'm busy.

Mavarara   Ha man, don't be this way. I haven't seen you for over a month. Every time I want to see you, you tell me you're busy. What's up? *Keng okare wanxomela yana?* [Why are you giving me the

	high hat (cold shoulder)?]
Thuli	*Ke bizi!* [I'm busy!] What must I do when I'm busy? I can't just leave my school work for you.
Mavarara	*Ha wena okare wa jola wena!* [Why do I get a sense that you're seeing someone else?] What? Have you found somebody else?
Thabo	*(To THULI)* Look, I'll just wait over there, if you still want me to help you with your books.
Mavarara	*Eintlek wena o mang?* [Actually, who the hell are you?]
Thabo	*Nna?* [Me?]
Mavarara	*(Mimicking him) Nnywa?* [Me?] Yes, you! Who the fuck are you?!
Thuli	Leave him alone.
Mavarara	*Keng?* [What?] Are you fucking her?! Is that why she's giving me the cold shoulder nowadays?
Thuli	Just leave him alone. Why don't you just leave before I call my mother?… I told you I'm busy. Just –
Mavarara	*(Taking out his gun) Voetsek! Tshek, sfebe!* [Fuck you! Fuck you, bitch!] You think I'm scared of your mother? I'm sick and tired of this! *Hoe lank ke go jola o sa ntshe fokol?! Kante o twatwaziwa ke dinaai tsa di foureyes.* [How long have I been seeing you without you putting out anything – only to find out that you're being fucked by this four-eyed idiot?] I've been patient and patient, understanding when you told me you're not ready for sex yet. It's been too long now! Too long.
Thabo	Leave her alone!
Mavarara	*Fok jou, jou fokon gamors!* [Fuck you, you fucking piece of shit!]

He turns with the gun to THABO and shoots. It is a spur of the moment thing. THABO is shot in the shoulder and falls to the floor.

There is a moment of silence as MAVARARA realises what he has done. He turns to THULI.

Mavarara   You see now what you made me do? Yeh? You see now?

All of a sudden, THABO jumps at MAVARARA from behind and grabs him by the neck.
Music.
They struggle for a while for the gun. The gun goes off, but THABO doesn't let go. He strangles MAVARARA, who finally dies.
THABO moves away from him and sits on a chair, thoughtful. THULI checks MAVARARA's breathing.
Music fades.

Thuli   He's dead.

She collapses beside MAVARARA's body and sits in silence… THABO moves towards the audience.

Thabo   *(To the audience)* We didn't report it. We buried the body.

She moves to him as she says:

Thuli   It was all my idea.
Thabo   No one reported him missing.
Thuli   He was a criminal who lived alone. He was no longer in touch with his family back in Limpopo.
Thabo   His friends assumed he had gone back to Limpopo and never bothered any more about him. It was a perfect killing.

He holds THULI in a loving manner as he says:

Thabo   From then on, Thuli and I, we shared a very deep,

dark secret... It was a secret bond that would
keep us together forever... Yes – we stayed
together, even after what happened later.

They move off with the body as the patrons pour into the shebeen.
Music.

BEAT THREE

It is late at night. The patrons are at their tables in the shebeen. DAN,
very drunk, slowly gets on top of the table.

Dan   People, lend me your ears... (*Lungi, who is*
seated drunkenly on one table, is alarmed when
he notices what Dan is doing.) If I was a white
man, I would say "drinks for everybody on the
house" like they do it in the movies... but – and a
big BUT – I'm broke and blue... blue and broke.

He laughs.

Lungi   *Mgan' wam'* [My friend] please get off the table!
Dan   *Bathong ke nale mathata.* [People, I have
problems.] My life is nothing but hell.
Lungi   Dan stop it, man! What is this? You're making
yourself a laughing stock... If you're drunk, why
don't you go home and sleep?
Dan   I have no home, bot... A home is not a home
without a child or a wife. This is my home.
Where's Mamiki? Mamiki?! *Okae?!* Mamiki?!

MAMIKI comes through again.

Dan   Mami – (*Notices her*) Oh yes... I was just telling
everybody... Your home is my home. This place
is my home. The Spanish say, *Mikasa sukasa*: "my
home is your home". But I don't have a home. So

	you should say that to me. Come on, say it…
	Mikasa sukasa.
Lungi	Dan please, man…
Dan	Lungi, you know my problems –
Lungi	Dan come down, please man. *Fuluga tafuli eo!* [Get off the that table.]
Dan	*(Laughs and mimicks Lungi)* "*Fuluga tafuli eo!*" Your Tswana is bad, my friend.
Mamiki	*Dan, ake o fologe mowe tuu! Otlo nkobela di-customer.* I've heard enough *ke di story tsa gago. Ha re di-social worker rona… Fologa wa senya!* [Dan, get off there, please. You're scaring my customers. I've heard enough of your stories, I'm not a social worker. Get off, you'll break my table.]
Dan	Are going to give me one more round?
Mamiki	If you don't get off there, I'm not going to bring it.
Dan	Okay, okay, my dol… Look, I'm getting off…

He gets off the table. MAMIKI disappears to the back.

Dan	*(To LUNGI)* Lulu?
Lungi	Huh?
Dan	Lungeee?

He gets off and plays around with LUNGI by tickling him.

| **Lungi** | Stop it, man… |

DAN has a moment with himself, it is as if a very depressing thought hits him…

| **Dan** | *(Introspectively) Goa nnyewa bot.* [Life is shit my friend.] |
| **Lungi** | I don't understand you *mgane wam'*… [my |

friend] I told you already, you have to deal with this boy… You can't get your wife back, but your daughter, you can! All you have to do is what I told you. *(Tries to be discreet)* You have to take your life into your hands now… do something… deal with this boy. This boy can't treat you like this and you let him live. Besides, it's the only way to get your daughter back. Mhlaba is not a guy to be messed with. He never fails. Never! *Phela hi nkabi loya.* [He's an *inkabi* – Zulu hitman – that man.]

Dan   I don't have money to pay him, man.

Lungi   I'll talk to him, don't worry. You'll pay him when you get a job.

DAN turns to the audience and addresses it.

Dan   Mhlaba was a Zulu guy from Natal. A very quiet loner Lungi had met in the shebeen. He was not a guy to be messed with. Rumour had it that he was an *inkabi*. *Inkabi* were Zulu hitmen who were famous for the many killings in the taxi industry. After Lungi talked to him about my situation… about that criminal boy Dario keeping my daughter as his prisoner, Mhlaba was more than happy to help…

Music.
We see the bleeding DARIO crawling across the front of the stage, dying. He is followed by a serene, panga-wielding MHLABA. DARIO dies slowly.

Dan   He didn't waste any time in killing Dario. It was as if he enjoyed doing it. Dario's murder was never solved… Even those people that might have seen Mhlaba doing the killing never told the police what they saw. Lungi tells me it's because people like Mhlaba are deeply connected to their ancestors. I don't know about that… all I know is, I was happy to have my daughter back with me again.

DAN and LUNGI walk out of the club. Mhlaba picks up the lifeless DARIO and starts walking off stage with him on his shoulder.

THABO and THULI are at their table. They kiss the way you find in black and white nineteen-twenties movies. Just then, MAMIKI comes in. She sees THABO and THULI kissing.

Mamiki	Thuli?! Thuli?! Thuli?!
Thuli	Mama?
Mamiki	How many times must I call you for you to hear me?
Thuli	*Sorry, a ka go kwa.* [Sorry, I didn't hear you.]
Mamiki	*O tla nkwa byang o nnetse banna.* [How can you hear me when you're focusing on men?]
Thuli	*Ha ka nn –* [I'm not –]
Mamiki	Shut up! There's school tomorrow, wash the dishes and go to sleep.
Thuli	Mare Mama I'm still talking to Thabo mos. I'll wash them later –
Mamiki	*Thuli, s'ka batla go ntena ntse ke tenegile, asemblief mosadi!* [Thuli, don't piss me off when I'm already pissed off, please woman!]
Thuli	Bye… I'll see tomorrow.
Thabo	Sure.

THULI leaves.

Mamiki	*(To THABO)* Can I talk to you?
Thabo	Sure…
Mamiki	Not here. In my bedroom…
Thabo	In your what?
Mamiki	You heard me.

She starts off and THABO follows her.

    Music for scene change. The bedroom is set up (but again such that we have both the shebeen area and MAMIKI's bedroom on stage).

BEAT FOUR

MAMIKI and THABO are in the bedroom area.

Mamiki	What are you doing?

Thabo	With what?

Mamiki	My daughter… Thuli. What are you trying to do?

He doesn't answer.

Mamiki	We talked about this. Didn't I tell you about this? I asked you to stay away from her. Didn't I?
Thabo	She's my girlfriend.
Mamiki	What are you – what do you mean she's your girlfriend?
Thabo	She's my girlfriend, I love her and she loves –
Mamiki	*(Going berserk)* Shut up, shut up, just shut up! She can't – that's my daughter there! What are you talking about?
Thabo	Look, I didn't want –
Mamiki	Will you just shut up! I mean, you – listen here, what… what about, what about us?
Thabo	Us?
Mamiki	Yes!
Thabo	There can't be "us" any more. I love her. I loved her even before we slept together… I loved her from the first time I saw her. It was… well, it was "love at first sight". Now she's my girlfriend… I love her and she loves me too, so you see… there can't be "us" any more, I can't do that to her.

Mamiki	Don't come and tell me rubbish! You sleep with me and then you want to fuck my daughter?! Do you think I'm just going to say, "go ahead, I give you my blessing"?! What game are you playing at? You can't fuck the both of us, I won't let it happen!
Thabo	It's not like that, it's not like that! I don't just want to fuck her! Don't you understand? I love her! She means everything to me! More than you or anyone can ever mean to me! She makes me – every, everything that is bad in me, she turns to good... Do you know what I mean? Do you even know what that feels like?!
Mamiki	I am taking this bitch away... I am taking her to her grandmother far, far away in the Limpopo where you won't find her.
Thabo	I thought you said she means everything to you? And now you're calling her a bitch?
Mamiki	Just get out of here, I don't even want to talk to you anymore!
Thabo	But –
Mamiki	Just go!

He starts off.

Mamiki   Thabo?!

He stops.

Mamiki   *(Tearful)* Wait! Please... don't go... I love you... Please, let's... let's just start from a clean slate and forget about all this... You stay away from Thuli and I will forget the whole thing ever happened. Just forget about her... Please... I know you're young... and she's also young, but... there's so many things I can give you that she won't be able to give you… I can give you anything you want… I have money… Huh?… I know it's not much, but it's enough… Just for the two of us… please… What do you say?

She kisses him. He says nothing and he doesn't resist and doesn't fall into the kiss.

Music.

She kisses him again, this time more passionately. He plays into it after a while. She moves him to the bed, trying to take control like the last time, but all of a sudden he reverses the power play and he takes control. He becomes aggressive. MAMIKI is impressed by this: she laughs with pleasure…

Mamiki   Oooh, I like that!

He is now on top of her. He takes off her red G-string and continues to kiss her before he strangles her. After MAMIKI dies, THABO gets off the bed and as he tries to wrap the body with a sheet, THULI enters. She is shocked at what she sees. There's a silent stand-off of horror between the two for a while. But as THABO tries to explain to THULI, reaching out to her, she runs off, screaming… He runs after her until he catches up with her in the shebeen area… They fall over as he grabs her.

Thabo   I had to do it. I had no choice. She was in the way, she was… she said she's take you away. *(Beat)* I can't… I can't lose you… You mean everything to me… When I'm with you, there's complete… peace within me… *(Beat)* You know, ever… ever since I started having this… this urge… to kill… to satisfy the raging nerves… I have always wanted that urge… that feeling to go away… But… I didn't know how… after meeting you, you made me feel good enough about myself for me to feel like stopping is… possible… Don't you see?… You're the air that I breathe…

He motions to kiss her, but she screams once again and runs off. He runs after her.
  Music for scene change.

BEAT FIVE

We are now at ROCKS MOTSHEGARE's house. ROCKS arrives home from work. He is surprised to find THABO in his house.

Rocks   Thabo?

THABO says nothing.

Rocks   Boy can you run. My running is not what it used to be nowadays. I ran after you the other day, at the shebeen, but you'd disappeared into thin air… like a phantom. *(Beat)* Anyway, howzit Bigboy? *(Beat)* It's been a long time. Where have you been? Huh? No call, no nothing. I've been very worried. I looked for you everywhere. Jesus, just look at how you've grown. How long's it been?
Thabo   Three years.
Rocks   You speak. For a minute there I thought you had lost your voice.

He laughs alone. THABO doesn't find that funny. ROCKS' smile fades.

Rocks   Well… uhm… how… What do you do now? Did you… did you continue with your schooling?
Thabo   I see the place still looks the same.
Rocks   Yep.
Thabo   And Mama's photos in the bedroom… they're still there.
Rocks   Yep.
Thabo   I thought you'd be married again by now.
Rocks   No, no, I love your mother too much to do that. I

	wouldn't – look, Bigboy, you want coffee or anything?
Thabo	I see her in my dreams, you know.
Rocks	Huh?
Thabo	And you too. The things you used to do to me, I have visions… terrible visions… The memories are strong.
Rocks	Well, uhm… you know, it's good to see you again, "the Great". I can't begin to tell you how –
Thabo	Do you hear me?
Rocks	What?
Thabo	I just told you… I have visions, vivid memories… of what you used to do to me.
Rocks	Come on, laytie, man… the past is the past… It's not good to bring out skeletons from the past… I'm…
Thabo	A changed man now?
Rocks	Yes.
Thabo	For you it's that easy, isn't it? Forget what you did to me. Just like that. As if –
Rocks	Look, what do you want?
Thabo	I want *you*! I want answers!
Rocks	Well, I don't have answers, Bigboy! I know how you feel but…
Thabo	*(Bursting out)* You don't know how I feel! You know NOTHING at all about how I feel!
Rocks	Easy, easy, boy… lower your voice…
Thabo	Why did you do it?!
Rocks	Look, I don't want to go back there! You're my son and I love you but… if that's all you came to talk about then you should just go!
Thabo	I'm not leaving here until I get answers. Why did you do it?
Rocks	Fuck off!
Thabo	Why did you do it?!
Rocks	I'm getting angry telling you the same thing

| | many times, boy. |
| **Thabo** | Why the fuck did you do it?! |

He grabs THABO in anger as if to crush him to pieces. THABO produces a gun from under ROCKS's chin. ROCKS freezes.

| **Thabo** | *(Calmly)* Move back! |

ROCKS takes a step back.

| **Thabo** | Again. |

ROCKS moves back again.

| **Thabo** | Take out your gun and throw it on the floor. |

ROCKS goes for his gun.

| **Thabo** | Slowly! Don't tempt me to shoot you. And I promise you, I will if you try any of your police tricks on me. |

| **Rocks** | Easy, Bigboy… Look… easy does it… Don't get excited. |

| **Thabo** | Take out your cuffs. |

He does.

| **Thabo** | Throw them here. |

He does.

| **Thabo** | Sit on the chair. |

He does. THABO moves behind the chair.

Thabo	Give me your hands.

ROCKS does and THABO cuffs him.

Thabo	Okay… now that we're relaxed, let's –
Rocks	This is too tight.
Thabo	Shut uuup!

Beat.

Thabo	I need answers… Give me answers. Why did you do that to me? Huh? Why? Why did you do that?
Rocks	Look, "the Great", uh…
Thabo	*(Going beserk)* Just stop it with that "the Great" shit! Just fuck it! I need answers here! *(Drawling angrily)* I need you to give me answers! Clear and tacit answers, none of your bullshit!
Rocks	I'm sorry, "the Great"…
Thabo	Fuck sorry! Do you have any idea of the pain you caused me?! Huh?! Do you have any idea?!
Rocks	Sorry, Bigboy…
Thabo	I was young, man! I was fucking young! I was just a child! You don't do that to a child! I asked you and I asked you to stop but you still went on! You went on without listening! I'm fucked up now! If it was only a matter of a painful arse and a few piles now and then, I'd understand – maybe I'd've long forgotten! But you tore my soul apart! And now I can't deal with the memories, I can't deal with the demons that are in my heart! And to deal with them, I go and kill… I rape and kill people…
Rocks	What are you telling me, Bigboy?! What do you mean?
Thabo	I don't want to kill any more… I want to be normal like other people…

He starts strangling his father.

Thabo   I want to stop… I don't want to kill anyone anymore…

The lights change and THABO's mother, MIHLOTI, appears…

Thabo   Mama?
Mihloti   Howzit, my baby?
Thabo   I'm fine. I'm going to be fine. I'm going to be fine now.
Mihloti   I miss you, my baby.
Thabo   I miss you too, Mama. Why did you have to die?! Why?!
Mihloti   That is not something you choose. It's something that just happens.

All this time ROCKS is choking like crazy – but THABO obviously has practice in strangling people, he is not even moving. He is crying and talking.

Thabo   But why did it have to happen to you?! Why you?! Why not him?! Why not him?! Why didn't he die in that car, Mama?!
Mihloti   It's no one's choice, my baby, it's something that just happens.
Thabo   I love you, Mama.
Mihloti   I love you too, my baby.

She walks off. The lights change back. ROCKS dies and stops kicking around.

Thabo   I love you, Mama… I love you very much.

THABO snaps out of his trance just when MOLOMO enters.

Molomo   Rocks?!

They both freeze.
   MOLOMO goes for his gun, but he clumsily lets it slip out of his hands to the floor – because of his fear. THABO goes for his own gun. MOLOMO tries to run away but is shot before he can get anywhere. THABO goes to him and checks whether he is still alive. He shoots again. He then comes back to centre stage and looks at the audience… Just when they expect him to say something, the lights change for the scene change…

EPILOGUE

The stage is now bare.
   We continue with a sequence that resembles the one the story began with, but now instead of SIBONGILE being the victim of the chase, it is MATLAKALA who is being chased around the stage. This time we see the chaser. It is THABO. He chases MATLAKALA until he catches her. He rapes her and strangles her with her G-string. When she is dead, he rises and addresses the audience. The sequence resembles the opening scene exactly.

Thabo   It's all just too fucking complicated. I didn't stop killing as I had thought I would. I still had the urge, I still had the feelings, the demons were still with me… I really did try to stop for a while but the feelings were just too strong. Now, I don't stress much about it… The way I look at it, it all depends on how you look at it… It's like the theory of relativity : "the appearance depends on where you're standing". From where *I'm* standing, this is necessary… It's all relative, really… I feel because I have a damaged soul, I am not wrong in doing this… The people that die, I no longer feel much for them… It's relative, I feel… If you look at it another way, through my eyes… these people are sacrifices to my demons... It's all like an indigenous African culture or society, where this tribe still sacrifice their virgins to the Gods. The West may get outraged all it wants to, but the tribesmen will never see anything wrong with it because it is their culture. It is what they believe in... So you see, things are all relative... It all depends on how you look at it... It's all relative.

He moves off.

A drunk LUNGI and DAN pass drunkenly in the background. They stop for a while and both pee.

Dan   Eish, bot, you know my daughter is going to kill me when she sees me like this. I promised her I wouldn't touch the bottle again.

Lungi   *I* didn't promise anything, nobody's going to kill *me*. But actually, I hate this veld, my friend... We'll get mugged to death here, let's go quickly.

Dan   I'm happy, bot. No one can kill me when I'm feeling like this. God is not that cruel. Why don't we both go to my place? I'm sure Matlakala has cooked one of those delicious recipes of hers.

Lungi   Eish, thank you, my friend... And *mina* I was going to eat a crust of dry brown bread before I sleep.

Dan   That's why it's great to have such a daughter, bot, come on.

They walk off singing drunkenly. The only light that remains on stage is the spotlight on the dead MATLAKALA. Blackout.

The End.

Biography

Mpumelelo Paul Grootboom

Paul is the 2005 recipient of the National Standard Bank Young Artist Award for theatre. He took up the position of Development Officer of the State Theatre in Pretoria after years of working with the North West Arts Council (now called the Mmabana Foundation). He is currently the dramaturge of the State Theatre.

Paul began his career as a writer for stage and television. His television writing credits include *Young Vision* (1994), *Suburban Bliss* (1995), *Isidingo* (2000), *Soul City* (2000), *Orlando* (2001) and *Mponeng*.

His other theatre writing credits include *Enigma* (1997), *Not With My Gun* (co-written with Aubrey Sekhabi, 1998), *Urban Reality* (1998), *Messiah* (1999), *The Stick* (co-written with Aubrey Sekhabi, 2000), *Dikeledi* (an adaptation of Sophocles' *Electra*, 2000), *Cards* (a re-writing of Mothusi Mokoto's script, 2002 and 2004) and *In this life* (co-written with Presley Chweneyagae, 2003).

He has directed theatre plays like *Urban Reality* (1998), *Dikeledi* (2000), *A Midsummer Night's Dream* (2001), *King Lear* (2002), *Cards* (2002 and 2004), *Hamlet* (2003), *Julius Caesar* (2003) and *In this life* (2003).

Presley Chweneyagae

Since his school years, Wesley has performed in numerous theatre productions for North West Arts. He has played Puck in *A Midsummer Night's Dream* and Zipper in *Cards* (Market Theatre, Grahamstown Festival, the State Theatre). In 2000, he was cast in a supporting role in *Orlando* for the SABC.

Presley recently achieved international recognition in the title role of the Oscar-winning film *Tsotsi*, an adaptation of Athol Fugard's novel.